WATER PARK

WATER PARK

ADAPTED BY TOM MASON & DAN DANKO

SCHOLASTIC INC.

New York   Toronto   London   Auckland   Sydney

Mexico City   New Delhi   Hong Kong

Based on the hit TV series created by Linwood Boomer.

Based on the teleplays "Water Park" by Maggie Bandur &
Pang-Ni Landrum and "Traffic Jam" by Dan Kopelman.

ISBN 0-439-22842-5

12 11 10 9 8 7 6 5 4 3 2 1   0 1 2 3 5 6/0
Printed in the U.S.A.
First Scholastic printing, November 2000

There are over 400,000 words in an unabridged dictionary, but ask any kid which one they hate the most and they'll give you the same answer: "homework." Of all the concepts created by Western civilization, that one compound word stinks the most. And if Eastern civilization thought of it first, it still stinks.

We kids have always had it bad. If we aren't getting up at five A.M. to milk the cows and feed the chickens, we're coming home at 3:30 to slave over homework. As if going to school seven hours a day, five days a week, nine months a year, twenty-one years straight (I am going to grad school), wasn't bad enough — I've got to come home and spend even more time preparing for the next day when the whole stupid thing starts over again?

What's my point? I don't know. Maybe I'd be happier milking cows?

That would be better than sitting in my room reading <u>Microscopic Parasites of the Serengeti: Friend or Foe?</u>

CHAPTER ONE

Twenty-four hours to go and we're outta here! Mom and Dad are taking us to Wavetown USA — the big water park. It's just water, slides, and no Krelboynes.

I'm ready to go, like, now, but my dad needs a day of preparation.

Mom slid the clippers along his hairy back with the skill of a race car driver. She clicked off the buzzing shears and admired her work.

"There you go, Hal," she said proudly. "All pink and shiny."

"Boys!" Dad called out.

Reese and I picked up two mirrors from the table. We held them behind Dad.

"I feel ten pounds lighter," Dad said, admiring his creamy-smooth and hairless back.

Some families have movie night or game night as bonding traditions. My family has "shave Dad's back." Usually, I don't look forward to it. I mean, who would? Right? I'm totally picking Dad hair off me for the next three days.

But for a trip to Wavetown USA? It's worth every hair-picking minute.

Dad braced himself against the table. Next came

the one thing I've never understood about shaving: the aftershave lotion.

Mom poured a full bottle of it into a washcloth and smacked it onto my dad's back.

"Hoo-hoo-hoo. That stings! Ha-ha-ha," Dad exhaled as the cloth was peeled away.

"Smooth as a seal," Dad enthused, a tone of pain lingering in his voice. "I'm ready for that waterslide."

Back in the '70s, my dad was one of the coolest kids in school. Too bad that was, like, forever ago. He's still stuck in that ancient time when bands had stupid names like "Foghat."

"We haven't had an outing in quite a while," Mom added as she tossed the empty aftershave bottle in the trash. "It's nice when we can do things together as a family."

Wait a second. Is this *my* family? Everyone is happy. Everything is going well. Everything is —

Dewey. I *knew* this was too easy.

Dewey's like a tiny wind-up toy whose switch is stuck on high gear. He never sits still, not even when he's asleep. If he's not flopping around, rolling around, or kicking, he's thinking about flopping around, rolling around, or kicking.

He wandered into the kitchen and slid his feet through the mounds of Dad's hair like Kristi Yamaguchi through a triple lutz.

"What's everybody doing?" Dewey asked.

Mom and Dad exchanged a look.

Trouble.

First there was Francis, and he got all the loving attention of both my parents. Then Reese came and took all that away, and Francis made sure that once Reese was old enough, he paid. Then I came along, and Reese made sure that I paid <u>twice</u> for all the times Francis made him pay once. Then Dewey was born, and it was my job as older brother to make him pay just like Reese had done before me and Francis before him. It was like handing down a family tradition.

That's the way of the big brother. In fact, they wouldn't be big brothers if they weren't punching, headlocking, or humiliating you.

I think that's why Dewey's always sticking things in his mouth and ears. He's coping with <u>three</u> older brothers. I decided to not make Dewey pay, so

Reese happily stepped up and took my place.

My heart really goes out to the little guy. Honest. But if Dewey blows this for us ... trust me ...

He'll pay.

CHAPTER TWO

"**W**HY CAN'T I GO?!"

Whoa. That got a ten on the "burst my eardrum" scale. And just to prove it wasn't a fluke the first time, he sucked in his two tiny lungs full of air and . . .

"WHY CAN'T I GO?!" Dewey bellowed again.

The oxygen expelled from his body, Dewey collapsed into Mom's lap like a kicked-over sand castle.

"We discussed this, honey," Mom said, her voice dripping with honey. "You have to stay home because of your ear infection."

"I never get to go," Dewey whimpered.

"I know it seems unfair, honey, but it's just this one time."

"And Disneyland," I reminded them. "And the chocolate factory. And the time we —" My third reminder was cut off by a sharp glare from you-know-who.

She looked back down at Dewey and brushed the hair from his forehead. "Maybe it's time you stop sticking dirty things in your ears."

Yeah. Especially *my* things.

Reese bounded into the room sucking on his pinky finger. He pulled it from his mouth and popped it into Dewey's ear.

"Hey, Dew, how's the ear?" He giggled.

Ever see one of those "Missing Link" photos in a tabloid? Well, if you shaved off all the hair, you'd have my older brother Reese. He even grunts like a monkey when he's eating. And let's just say that if I got twice the brains as everyone else in the family, Reese got half to balance everything out.

"Reese! Stop teasing him!" Mom spat out. "Remember, if your father doesn't find a baby-sitter, no one's going anywhere. We'll see who's crying then."

What?! We are at WP minus ten and counting and still no baby-sitter? So help me, if Dewey's ears screw up this trip to Wavetown, I'm plugging them with plaster.

"Oh, no, it's just the little one," Dad said into the phone to a potential baby-sitter. He desperately paced around the kitchen. "The other two aren't going to be anywhere near you. Promise."

It's hard to get a good sitter lately. You think maybe it's us?

I don't think we've ever had good luck with baby-sitters. Francis still laughs about the time he bit one with his first tooth. And then Reese and I locked one in the closet. He was really angry until he got scared of the dark. And that thing we found in the road that got one baby-sitter to run home crying? Awesome!

While *we* were dealing with Dewey's baby-sitter blues, far, far away Francis also found himself in a corner. A corner pocket, to be exact.

CHAPTER THREE

Marlin Academy is one of the finest military schools in Alabama. It may also be the only military school in Alabama. That's where my brother Francis was sent.

If you look up the word *cool* in the dictionary, you'll see a picture of Francis, all tall and blond. Of course, if you look up *delinquent*, you'll probably see his picture there, too.

Commandant Spangler casually strolled around the billiard table, assessing the position of the numbered balls. He stopped. With all the effort of a yawn, he sunk two striped balls into the side and corner pockets with one fluid shot.

"You'd think I'd get bored of wiping the floor with my cadets," Spangler said, chalking his cue.

"God knows *we* enjoy it, sir," Francis replied.

Francis and Spangler were facing off in the match-to-end-all-matches. A winner-take-all duel to the death. Okay, maybe not to the death, which is probably a good thing. Francis was getting his butt kicked.

I'm not sure, but I swear this Spangler sleeps in his military uniform. He's that tough. I think he's more parts than man, like Frankenstein's monster without the neck bolts. But he does have this really cool eye patch!

"Do you know what your problem is, cadet?" Spangler asked Francis as he sunk another ball.

Wherever we go in our lives, someone always wants to know if *we* know what our problem is. What's up with that?

"You may have mentioned it once or twice, sir," Francis said, rolling his eyes. "But I never tire of hearing it."

"Discipline," Spangler said, sinking a ball to emphasize his point. "Anything worth doing, son, is worth doing well. Whatever I do, whether it's teaching you boys, mastering tai chi, or playing billiards . . ." Spangler sized up the table. Only the eight ball remained. Spangler leaned over the table and propped his right arm in the middle, revealing a bridge attachment connected to the end.

Wow, a detachable hand! I don't know if that's cool or creepy. The way Francis always talks about this guy, I bet he keeps his real one in a jar next to his bed.

"I practice. I focus. I push myself," Spangler continued with the lecture as his billiard stick slid on the bridge. "But *you* don't commit to anything, son. You're never going to win because you do everything halfhearted."

Spangler shot for the eight ball, corner pocket. It would end the game. All of Francis's finger-crossing and jinxing couldn't stop the outcome. Or maybe it could. Spangler missed and Francis sighed in relief.

"Regrettable" was the only word Spangler said as the eight ball rolled off the cushion.

"You may have spoken a little too soon, sir. I think you'll find that I play this game with my whole heart." Francis smirked and confidently chalked his own cue. "Eight ball, corner pocket."

The shot was called. The stick slid gracefully between Francis's fingers like they were buttered. And maybe they were buttered, because the cue ball followed the eight ball down the corner pocket like Alice chasing the White Rabbit.

Francis grumbled and slumped on the table's edge.

"Ah, the fatal scratch," Spangler gloated. "Once again, I waltz away with Lady Victory. And until you focus, Francis, she will never be your dance partner."

Spangler put his arm around Francis and smiled. Maybe Spangler wanted to be Francis's dance partner?

CHAPTER FOUR

Yes! Wavetown day is here! And so's Dewey's baby-sitter. She looked like a cross between the Wicked Witch of the West and an M-1 tank. I mean, this woman was large enough to bend light. Her dress was like a flowered tent and her dull yellow hat matched the color of her teeth.

Oh well, that's Dewey's problem. I'm soon going to be sliding into temperature-controlled water.

"Mrs. White, thank you so much for coming over on such short notice," Mom gushed to the battle-ax. "It was nice of your agency to give us a second chance." Mom turned to Dewey and squeezed his shoulder tightly. "Honey, you two are going to have so much fun together," she said through gritted teeth and a stabbing smile. Dewey understood what she was really saying: "Don't you dare hurt her."

Dad honked the car horn and Reese bolted through the kitchen in a T-shirt. "Hurry! The sun's coming up!" he yelled and shot out the door. Mom and I quickly followed, leaving Dewey behind with his new warden.

"Want to play a game?" Dewey asked meekly.

Mrs. White leaned toward Dewey. Her large body blocked out the early morning sun like an eclipse. "No."

I felt bad for Dewey. Honest. We've all been there. Stick one too many things in your ear and there's going to be consequences. I'm just glad that today, my only consequence was sitting in the backseat, twelve miles from Wavetown USA.

We passed by a large billboard. It showed an apple-pie family laughing and happily playing together in the perfect waters of Wavetown.

Luckily, they let families like mine in, too.

"Why can't we go to Wild Rivers?" Reese whined as all of our eyes tracked the billboard. "They have better slides."

"Well, you should've thought of that before you got us banned for life," Dad responded.

Man, did Reese get us banned for life. It was two years ago and he — no, I better not say. What he did was so bad, just thinking about it causes trouble.

"Wavetown is fine. They finally got rid of that algae bloom," Dad continued. He checked his teeth in the rearview mirror, then added, "Hey, Malcolm, think you'll go down the Liquidator this time?"

"Don't pressure the boy, Hal," Mom swooped in to defend.

"I wasn't pressuring. I just —"

"He's scared enough without you making a big deal out of it."

Why is it that parents always think they can talk about you as if you aren't there? Like them acting as if I weren't there while they listed my neuroses in detail somehow prevented humiliation.

"Hey, I'm not scared," I quickly said, hoping none of them would realize how scared I was.

"Of course not, honey. We believe you," Mom said in the same voice she usually reserved for Dewey.

Great. No one believed me.

Why is so much of childhood designed to scare the heck out of you? When we're little, our parents read us stories about gingerbread houses made of baked children and nasty trolls living under broken-down bridges. I think it's their revenge because we took away their Saturday nights.

The funny thing is, once we get old enough to stop being scared by those bedtime stories, what do we do? We go look for bigger things to scare us more.

Rides. Movies. Girls.

But I've got to ride the Liquidator. I don't have a choice. I chickened out the last time we came here and had to face the endless sarcasm, laughter, and finger-pointing.

Until Mom finally made Dad stop.

CHAPTER FIVE

As we left the car and entered Wavetown, I tied my swim trunks extra tight. One hundred yards of water slide is a force not to be trifled with. The last thing I needed was to come out at the bottom several seconds after my trunks.

I thought that was my biggest worry. I thought wrong.

"What are you smiling about?" I asked Reese. And he *was* smiling that stupid dork grin of his.

"Nothing," he replied.

Right. It's never nothing with him. Reese was definitely up to something. The only question was, was my role accomplice? Or target?

"Hey, Mom . . . ?" Reese began.

Target.

"Isn't Malcolm supposed to wear his nose plug for his sinuses?"

A sneak attack. Unbelievable! My guard was down and Reese took full advantage of the opening.

"Shut up!" I hissed at him, but it was too late. His plan was in motion like a snowball rolling down a hill.

"Oh yeah, that's right," Mom said, turning to me.

"Oops. I forgot it," I quickly replied. Yeah. Forgot it on purpose. Maybe she wouldn't call me on it. Or worse, have a spare in her tote bag.

"Well, just be careful, then," Mom warned.

Whew. That was a close one. I thought I was going to face the humiliation of —

"Don't worry, here it is," Reese snickered as he dangled the nose plug in my face.

Ouch! That hurt worse than any nose plug! Reese hit so far below the belt, he was punching my kneecaps. Now I have to spend the whole day with my nose pinched together, sounding like a human kazoo. And the elastic band that goes around my head? Makes my ears stick out like a jumbo jet. I will not wear this thing. It's off the moment Mom's gone.

"Don't think you can take off that nose plug as soon as I'm gone. You have to wear it all day. And I want to see the dents in your nose," Mom commanded.

How does she do that? My mom is like a steamroller with longer hair. Once she gets started you either jump on board or get run over. I saw a movie once where some kid said the chill you get on the back of your neck is from ghosts. No way. It's from one of my mom's lectures.

"But I'm not even in the water yet," I protested in my nose-plugged voice.

"You'll lose it. That nose of yours has cost us too

much money already. If I see you for one second without that plug, you'll spend the day in the Kiddie Sprinkler."

First she throws me in the Krelboyne class at school. And now she threatens me with the Kiddie Sprinkler? Did she take courses in ruining my life? Or does it come naturally?

Well, the joke's on her. My life is *already* ruined.

I watched Mom and Dad leave, and then I heard it. Screams. From above me, torsos twisted and turned through long black tubes. The sound of surging water propelling bodies like human bullets thundered above me. The Liquidator: Niagara Falls in a tube.

The Kiddie Sprinkler wasn't looking so bad right now.

"Okay, what should we do first?" Reese asked, completely oblivious to my anger.

"What makes you think I want to do anything with you?" I spat back. Even my nose plug couldn't pinch the resentment out of my voice.

"What's your problem?" Reese replied.

"That nose plug thing was bogus. You crossed the line, Reese."

"What?" I wasn't sure if Reese was asking me a question, or still didn't understand that I was ballistic.

"You sold me out to Mom. It would be different if I had done something to you, but it was totally cold-blooded."

"Don't be such a baby." Reese shrugged.

"What you did was an act of war! And believe me, I *will* get you back. You won't know where or when, but you're going to pay!" I yelled. My voice imploded through my nose, making it sound like a hollowed-out watermelon. Reese stared at me for a moment.

Did my threat work?

"Heh-heh," he laughed and pointed at me. "You sound funny."

If this isn't the most humiliating moment of my life since I became old enough to control my bladder, I don't know what is.

I hope Reese enjoys the moment, because I meant what I said. Somehow, someway, I will get him back. Today. My vengeance shall be swift and merciless, like the jumbo burrito from the Taco Hut.

Of course, sometimes I wonder if Reese and I will ever grow out of our unspoken oath to destroy each other's childhood. It seems that no matter where we are or what we're supposed to be doing, unless there's an easier target, we always aim at each other.

I think maybe it's time I leave all that childishness behind, you know? Turn over a new leaf and all that.

I totally think that's what I'll do. Act mature. Act grown-up. Do the right thing.

Right after I get even with that creep.

CHAPTER SIX

Francis stood outside Commandant Spangler's door, running through all the possible things he might have done wrong in the last week. If Francis could narrow it down to a few, he could create a defense. But the list was too long. Francis gave in and knocked on the door.

"Enter," Spangler's voice boomed from the other side.

"You wanted to see me, sir?" Francis said meekly as he sat in the chair across from Spangler.

"I just got a call from the sheriff," Spangler said. He took his good hand and ran it the length of his bald head.

Maybe he was checking for new hair?

"Seems a smug, smart-mouthed youth looking very much like yourself has been hustling billiards in the local bars."

"Really, sir?" Francis was buying time. Mere seconds of planning could be the difference between Plausible Excuse and Obvious Lie.

"You're in serious trouble, cadet."

"I can explain everything —"

"I am *furious* with you," Spangler thundered, rising

to his feet to stand over Francis. "Why have you been holding back when we play billiards?"

"What?" Francis was shocked.

"I want to know why you've been letting me win."

"Oh, sir, if I played for real, I would just end up beating you, and you'd lose face in front of the cadets," Francis answered, like he had to explain everything to Spangler. "And we know how much you'd hate that. Then you'd punish all of us. Really, no good can come from it, sir. Besides, winning seems to make you so happy."

"I'm not a child." Spangler's voice deepened with anger. "I can't believe you and the other cadets have been making a mockery of me."

"Oh no, sir. They really *do* stink. I'm the only one making a mockery of you."

Oops. *That* didn't come out right.

"Do you really think me so petty that I would throw a tantrum over something as small as a game of billiards?" Spangler yelled, beginning to throw a tantrum.

"My mistake, sir."

"I want your best game, cadet. And to make sure of that, if you don't win . . ." Spangler paused and smiled. An authority figure smiling? That's *never* good.

"Picture yourself at oh-four-hundred," Spangler continued, "awakened from sweet dreams of Mommy and sent out into the bitter cold to raise our school colors and stand at attention until reveille is called three hours later. . . . Now picture that for the next two hundred and thirty consecutive days."

Francis pictured it. It was as ugly as any school photo. "What if I try my best and still lose?"

"Then you shall be miserable indeed," Spangler replied. "Dismissed."

CHAPTER SEVEN

There's something about sand and water that makes parents go mushy in the brain. I think it's the repetitive splashing of the artificial-wave generator. My mom and dad were no exception. I saw them sitting beneath a plastic palm tree, their toes dangling in the chlorinated water.

"Remember, honey, how I promised you that exotic island vacation," Dad said, putting his arm around Mom. "But we had to go and have kids instead?"

"Mmm-hmm," Mom dreamily responded.

"Well, I was thinking maybe today could be our little island getaway. We have the sun, the sand, the palm trees. And I brought some treats."

Dad held out a paper bag of candy bars and wagged it in front of my mom's eyes. "We're not paying those concession stand prices."

"Oh, Hal," Mom gushed. "You're so cute when you sneak in junk food."

Eww. I was getting a sick feeling in the pit of my stomach, and it wasn't from my two chili dogs. Then I saw Reese standing in the food line. Time to strike.

"Hey, Reese," I said, coming up behind him. "I think

I saw that girl you like. The one with the brown hair, kinda curly."

"April?" Reese's eyes widened with anticipation.

"April. Yeah, that's her." Time to place the bait. "Why'd you say you like her again?"

"Well." Reese beamed. "I think she has a crush on me."

Reese was so predictable.

"Is that true, April?" I said, turning to the girl who stood directly behind Reese.

Reese spun around and stood face-to-face with April. Her mouth was open, awaiting a scream, but she was too shocked. Or horrified. She glared at Reese for a moment, then stormed away.

Too easy. My revenge was complete.

"Now we're even," I sneered.

Reese lunged for me and I ran. He chased me across the mini-beach, kicking up sand like a crazy gopher. People yelled and shouted as we bolted past the lifeguard post and back into the crowd of water-park-goers.

After a few slippery twists and turns, I finally lost Reese. He was still out there, waiting for me to show myself. But I wasn't going to let my creep brother keep me from enjoying the water rides.

Only then did I realize I was standing under *the* water ride. Once more, the screams echoed from above me. I was under the Liquidator. Oh well, if this ride didn't kill me, Reese would, so I had nothing to lose. And I can do this. No one here cares whether I do it or not. No big deal.

I made my way up through the line. At each turn was a new sign warning of bodily injury. DANGER! ACHTUNG! PELIGRO! So I'm supposed to be more excited about the ride because they show me a checklist of possible injuries? Maybe having full use of all your limbs is overrated.

I looked up the rickety, winding staircase that led into the clouds and to the twisting black tube of torture. I slouched as I passed the YOU MUST BE THIS TALL TO RIDE sign.

"Straighten up, son," the attendant said as he measured me against the sign.

Slowly, I straightened up. Did I say slowly?

"See? You're well clear," the attendant said happily.

"Great."

"Now move along. You're holding up the line."

I gripped the railing and started climbing. One foot. Another foot. Maybe this wasn't going to be so bad.

Then I heard the screams. The screams of others as they hurtled down the Liquidator. I convinced myself they were screams of happiness.

"Please keep your arms and legs crossed at all times," the pimply-faced attendant warned each slider. "Do not bend your legs. Do not lift your head. Remove all piercings. You may not wear anything around your neck. We are not legally liable for any injury which may result." He paused. "Enjoy the ride."

There. I made it to the top. It just takes one more little step. One ... tiny ... step ... into ... the ... black ... hole. I'll just rock forward and slide down on three. And it'll all be over.

"One!" Rock.

"Two." Rock.

"Three!"

I jumped out and headed for the wussy exit.

Okay. So that didn't go *exactly* the way I planned. Instead of being shot out the bottom in a wave of triumph, I skulked all the way back down the staircase. Each person in line stared at me. Would I rather face this humiliation than ride the Liquidator? Amazingly, I passed kids half my age and adults twice my parents'. Some pointed and laughed, but most just shook their heads in silence.

Halfway through my march of shame, I saw Reese in line, going up. I knew he saw me, but I hoped if I hung my head low enough, he might feel sympathy for the first time in his life.

What? I can hope.

"Hey there, girlie," Reese sneered. "Let me adjust your bra strap."

Reese reached out and pulled the nose plug off my nose. He stretched it back like a slingshot and released it. The nose plug shot toward my face and smacked me in the eye.

"Now we're even." Reese laughed.

So much for hope.

CHAPTER EIGHT

They had been staring at each other forever, or at least five minutes, which was probably the longest Dewey had ever done any one thing in his life.

Mrs. White's breaths were deep and rhythmic. In. Out. In. Out. Dewey's were quick and shallow like a panting rabbit.

He stared at Mrs. White for a few moments longer and then finally asked, "Can I watch TV?"

"No," Mrs. White responded, pausing in mid-inhale.

Dewey watched Mrs. White's nostrils flair with each breath. It was hypnotic and Dewey found himself drifting off into a relaxed mellowness.

Then Dewey remembered he was bored.

"Can I play video games?" Dewey asked.

"No," Mrs. White responded, this time on an exhale, so it came out with a hiss.

Dewey looked around the room. Not much happening there. He turned back to Mrs. White.

"Can we read a book?"

"No."

"Can I —"

"No."

Dewey scratched his head.

This was a trick adults played sometimes. I call it "Guess Again." See, the adult knows there's no right answer, but they make you keep guessing. They must get some warped thrill from it.

"What can I do?" Dewey asked, finally giving up.

"Something quiet," Mrs. White said.

Quiet? Dewey doesn't even *sleep* quietly. Dewey picked up a green toy car and rolled it gently across the table.

"Quieter," Mrs. White ordered.

Dewey picked up the car and drove it on an invisible freeway several inches above the table. If today didn't stop Dewey from sticking things into his ears, nothing would.

After several dull seconds of watching "Green Car and the Freeway in the Sky," Mrs. White walked over to the kitchen table and emptied out a container of . . . buttons?

Yup, buttons. Green ones, blue ones, square ones, three-hole ones, and just plain button ones. Adults collect the lamest things. What is it with them? Like, one day when they're old, they totally get a craving and say to themselves, "Gosh, I think I'll start collecting shoelaces."

Mrs. White slid a button from the large pile to a smaller pile. Then she reached into the center of the massive Mt. Button and picked one off the peak. This one she dropped into a new pile.

Dewey picked up a lone button near the edge of the table and dropped it on the first pile.

"No, no, no," Mrs. White chastised. "First we sort by holes, *then* by color."

Sort by holes, then by color? Does *that* sound fun, or what?

Dewey watched Mrs. White sort by holes one more time, then worked up enough courage to try again. He pulled a button with six holes from the mountain and plopped it onto a small mound of similar-holed buttons.

"That's better," Mrs. White said, scrutinizing his every sort.

His self-confidence swelling from Mrs. White's approval, Dewey reached for a new button, this time trying a four-holer. His newfound sorting enthusiasm was interrupted when Mrs. White grabbed his wrist.

"What's in your mouth?" she asked, glaring into his eyes.

"Nothing," Dewey mumbled.

"There are at least twenty things I won't tolerate. And one of them is lying," she said and placed her hand under Dewey's mouth. That's pretty daring. I've seen what can come out of there.

Dewey looked around the room, hoping something would suddenly swoop in and save him. As usual, nothing happened. He reluctantly yielded the prize in his mouth.

"You're eating my buttons?" Mrs. White gasped as the spit-covered button plopped into her hand.

"Not eating, saving," Dewey corrected.

"Are you a hamster? What were you saving it for?"

"I don't know." Dewey shrugged. "It's pretty. It's my favorite one."

Mrs. White inspected the button. "Actually," she confessed, "this is my favorite, too." She reached into the large pile and pulled out another button. "What do you think of this one?"

"It's ugly," Dewey said, scrunching his face. "I hate it."

"Me too," Mrs. White whispered conspiratorially. "My, you're a smart little boy."

Dewey looked up at Mrs. White and smiled. Maybe she'd let him watch TV after all.

CHAPTER NINE

"**M**om! Make Reese stop!" I shouted as I ran up to Mom and Dad at the fake beach. "He's being a total jerk. He's ruining everything and —"

My mom and dad stopped kissing and both of them glared at me.

"Malcolm, does it look like I am open for business?" Mom yelled back. "You've done nothing but pester us. Is it too much to ask that your father and I enjoy one *day*?"

Open for business? I didn't even know parents closed. It should be a 24/7 job and now that I need them to stop Reese, they're more concerned about relaxing?

"But Reese is —" I tried to go for the "please help me" whine.

"I don't want to hear it," Mom interrupted. "You either take care of it yourself or you two get locked up in the car for the rest of the day. I mean it."

This stinks.

Then I spotted Reese. He was in the wave pool obnoxiously splashing the people next to him and chortling like an idiot. The welt under my eye smarted for a second. I still owed Reese for the nose plug snap.

"Help! My brother can't swim!" I yelled to the lifeguard and pointed at Reese.

In a flash, the lifeguard leaped from his tower and was on top of Reese like a bad smell. Reese kicked and screamed. He had no clue why this large man was dragging him toward the edge. He gulped a few mouthfuls of water. Reese was totally acting like a drowning kid. The lifeguard tightened his grip and dragged him out of the water.

Reese flopped onto his back like a dead fish.

"Give him some air, people!" the lifeguard shouted to the gathering crowd.

Reese groggily opened his eyes just in time to see the wide-open mouth of the lifeguard swoop down on him. Reese's eyes bulged like balloons as the lifeguard began mouth-to-mouth CPR.

Even *I* hadn't expected that. It's great when an already devious plan delivers unforeseen benefits.

I looked over the lifeguard's shoulder. "Now we're even," I said to Reese as his shouts were muffled by the lifeguard's second round of CPR.

CHAPTER TEN

If you ask me, billiards is a stupid game. Nothing blows up. Nothing transforms. Nothing comes back from the dead. You just take a long stick and poke it at numbered balls. Yawn. The only cool thing about billiards is slamming the cue ball really hard to see if you can hit somebody standing too close to the table.

But to Francis, it's an art. He's not one for school, but a billiard table is his mecca. The only English he enjoys learning is the one he puts on a cue ball.

Francis examined the table. He calculated trajectories and angles, cued up, and sunk two balls as the other cadets watched.

"You seem to be practicing pretty hard," cadet Joe said as the seven ball thunked into the pocket before him. "I hope you're not planning on doing something stupid." He paused. "Like winning."

Francis stood from the table. "Look, guys, I know you want me to lose, but Spangler demanded I play a real game."

"You can't win, Francis," cadet Pete insisted. "If you do, Spangler will take it out on us."

"Remember when Hendrix beat him playing

HORSE on a lucky shot?" Pete asked. "We couldn't watch anything on TV except PBS for a whole week."

"And it was during pledge drive," Joe added mournfully.

Francis shook his head. "Do you know what Spangler's going to do to me if I lose?"

"Do you know what *we're* going to do to you if you win?" Joe threatened and took a menacing sip from his PBS mug.

Spangler cleared his throat and the cadets parted like the Red Sea. "Are you ready for our showdown?" Spangler challenged Francis.

Francis gave a brief look at the pack of seething cadets surrounding the table and let out a long sigh. "Let's get this over with."

The games were tight and fast, and after four, it was tied two each. Francis sunk two consecutive shots and buckled down for the eight ball kill. He took the shot, but the cue ball gently touched the corner, missing the target. The cadets let out a unified sigh of relief.

"Sorry, sir," Francis said, as if he should apologize for not winning.

"Understandable, cadet," Spangler said, chalking his cue. "I've seen professionals do much worse. I guess the billiard gods are smiling on me today."

Spangler leaned over the table to take a shot. The cue ball shot off his cue, missed the three ball, and accidentally sunk the eight ball. Spangler lost the game amid a wave of groans from the cadets.

"Then again, the billiard gods can be fickle. I guess you won that round, cadet."

"What are you doing?" Francis whispered to Spangler.

Spangler leaned past Francis's head and checked the "games won" markers. "I think I'm losing. And gracefully, I'd like to point out."

"But you could've made that shot."

"I could say the same to you." Spangler was perturbed. "There were at least a dozen shots you held back on. And since you seem to be more motivated to lose, I'm going to beat you at your own game."

"Huh?" It came out of Francis's mouth as more of a choke than a word.

"I'm going down, son. I'm going down hard," Spangler said, breaking a grin.

"But sir," Francis protested, "the guys will kick my butt if I win."

"Well, that's just gravy. May the best man lose."

Spangler patted Francis on the back and limped back to the billiard table to break for the next game. Francis watched in horror as Spangler took the opening shot and sunk the eight ball.

"Oh fudge, I seem to have scratched again," Spangler said and offered Francis a cruel smile. "Looks like you're on a roll, cadet."

Francis looked at the cadets, who ominously

leered back. At that moment, Francis realized there was only one thing to do: lose like he's never lost before.

It was Francis's turn to break, and following Spangler's lead, he sunk the eight ball on the opening shot and lost the game.

"Looks like that one goes to you, sir," Francis smugly said to Spangler.

The games flew by fast and furious, Francis and Spangler doing everything within their power to lose. Three-cushion ricochets, spinning English, cue balls curving, back-spinning, and jumping over other balls to knock the elusive eight ball into the pocket. It was an impressive display of incredible skills entirely focused on losing.

Nobody wants to lose, but then nobody wants to get beaten up by fifteen military cadets, either. And in the end, no one really cared who won or lost. Everybody cheered with each new trick shot by Francis and Spangler until both players hung up their billiard sticks for the day and shook hands.

"Good playing, cadet," Spangler said.

"Same to you, sir," Francis said, happy to sleep beyond 0400 hours and without a butt-kicking.

CHAPTER ELEVEN

Okay. So you hear all that laughing? Can you feel the fingers point? That's right. I went to the top of the Liquidator a second time.

And for a second time, I chose the wussy exit.

So I chickened out. What? *You've* never been afraid?

I climbed down the wussy exit doing my best to ignore the pointing and laughing. I passed some small children, two middle-aged women, a couple of old men in Speedos. They were all staring at me, the chicken.

"Hey look, it's that nose plug kid," some scrawny boy pointed out just before he took a big wheeze on his inhaler.

Sigh. I give up.

I took my shame and meandered over to my dad. I ripped the nose plug off my face, threw it down in disgust, and plopped next to him.

"Before you say anything, Malcolm," Dad immediately began, "I just want to tell you, I don't want to hear it. Can't you give your mother and me five minutes of peace?"

"You know what?" I spat out, lying back in a final collapse of defeat. "You can have the rest of the day, because I give up. I'm not gonna have *any* fun, so why try?"

"As long as we're on the same page." Dad got up, wiped the sand from his legs, and left.

Everything stinks. I've done nothing but chicken out, get laughed at, and fight with Reese. I was just going to lie down, enjoy the sun, and wait for them to take me home when this hideous day is finally over.

I closed my eyes.

Splat.

I opened my eyes.

First of all, I don't even know where Reese would *find* an athletic supporter, but somehow he did and now it was laying across my face.

Across my *face!*

I pulled it off and threw it to the side. Reese stood over me.

"*Now* we're even." He laughed and ran off to the Slideaway.

That was it. I'd had enough. Nose plugs. Liquidators. Athletic supporters. I was going to end this here and now. I snuck up behind Reese as he stood in line for the Slideaway. There was only one thing to do, and I did not hit *pause.*

I grabbed Reese's swim trunks and yanked them down to his ankles.

The crowd around Reese gasped, but no one

gasped louder than April, who stood directly in front of the totally humiliated Reese.

There have been many times in my young life that I have done something that I immediately regretted. Pulling down Reese's trunks in front of April?

What was I thinking?!

Reese's body trembled. His eyes twitched. His face twisted like a pretzel. I didn't stick around long enough to hear what his scream sounded like.

I made a mad dash for freedom, but Reese was out for blood. He had crossed the line earlier, but I smashed that line and danced on its tiny pieces.

I ran blindly through the park, dodging and weaving between people like Han Solo flying through an asteroid field. Unfortunately, I hit one: asteroid Mom.

I didn't mean to. I plowed into my parents as they left the food stand. Because I didn't break stride, Dad was now covered in nachos and hot dogs and Mom was wearing a full coat of soda.

"Boys!" Mom screamed at the top of her lungs.

The pursuit continued. Soon I was out of places to run, so I bolted up the Liquidator line. I could hear the angry growls of Reese as he closed the distance between us.

"I've done some soul searching, Reese, and I understand now that I stepped over the line!" I called back, hoping to reason with the raging beast. "And I feel you might think that we're far from even, but I just wanted you to know how truly sorry I am! It was very wrong of me! And I'm not just saying that because I'm running out of space and you're going to kill me."

And then, I ran out of space. I was at the front of the line. Of the Liquidator.

"Hey! There's no cutting!" the attendant said at the top of the ride. Then he saw it was me, Mr. Wussy Exit himself. He rolled his beady eyes. "Oh, it's you again."

I ignored his mocking words. I had to deal with Reese. "I am so sorry, Reese," I pleaded. "I really, really mean it." Two "reallys" should do it.

Reese didn't care what I really, really meant. All Reese cared about was hurting me. Badly. He cocked his fist.

I couldn't fight Reese. Well, I could, but it wouldn't make any difference. Fighting just came too naturally to him. If I did land a blow, it would only make him madder. So I prepared to take my punishment and silently prayed for Reese to have a seizure.

And he was seized all right. By Mom. She had climbed up the Liquidator after us. She grabbed Reese's wrist and spun him around like a human top.

"Do you think we're wealthy?" she asked.

There we were, standing at the top of the Liquidator, an angry line of people behind us and a perturbed attendant in front of us. Given the situation, I wasn't so much surprised by Mom's question, but by the shocking level of calmness in her voice.

"What?" I said.

"Do you think we're wealthy?" Mom asked in the same mellow voice.

Reese and I looked at each other and shrugged.

I don't remember lighting a fuse, but there sure was one heck of an explosion. From Mom.

"Wealthy people drive fancy cars! They buy fresh pasta!" she erupted at Reese and me. She was like a volcano in a bathing suit. "Do we do any of those things? No! Those people can afford to have their vacations ruined! No big deal. They just turn around and go again. Your father and I work so hard and so long. What is wrong with you two? Are you aborigines? Sane children would appreciate a trip to the water park! They would have fun! We don't go enough places for you to ruin them!"

Mom stopped and finally took a breath. Reese and I lifted our heads. I started to speak, but she finished inhaling and began round two.

"Every time I turn around, I hear screaming and fighting. I keep hoping that it's someone else's children, but no, it's always you two! There are swimming pools! There are water slides! This isn't enough to keep you occupied? You have to keep going at each other like rabid monkeys? You can do that any day, but you just have to make me suffer, don't you?"

She didn't end there. She wanted to make her point. And then make a point of her point. I don't mean to be disrespectful, but at a certain stage, parents' yelling just starts sounding like static on the

TV. Their lips are moving, the sound's coming out, but I've long ago turned to another station.

And the station I turned to this time was my mom's feet. I realized she was standing in the little launch area of the Liquidator. I used my eyes to signal Reese.

Reese's eyes followed mine and saw the same thing. He immediately threw me a "no way" look.

I was at the crossroads. Reese's beating or Mom's wrath.

At a certain time in every young man's life, he must face the same decision: "Should I or shouldn't I?" The situations will always be different, the level of risk varied, but the question is always the same. "Should I or shouldn't I?" These moments must never be entered into hastily. The possible outcomes must be analyzed and pondered. Rash decisions must not be made, for they could affect the remainder of a person's —

Oh, what the heck. I pushed her.

Her arms waved in the air as she tried to regain her balance, with no luck. Mom flopped on her back and into the tube.

"Arms and legs crossed at all times!" the attendant yelled down the tube.

Reese's mouth fell to the floor. Any memory of his anger was washed away with our mother. "Dude, that was the bravest thing I've ever seen."

"Yeah."

"You're gonna die," Reese said, almost as nervous as I was.

"I know," I replied and looked down the tube. "Do you think she's okay?"

She was more than okay. She was hungry for revenge. Mom's hand thrust out from the darkness of the Liquidator tube. She grabbed Reese and me and yanked us into the black tube after her.

The three of us plummeted into the darkness, screaming every watery, liquidating inch of the way.

I can't believe I did that. It doesn't matter if I survive the Liquidator. Mom'll kill me. And it's really tough thinking of excuses while you're plummeting through a dark tunnel of twisting doom.

"Sorry, Mom, I slipped."

"It wasn't me!"

"I was trying to hug you."

Wow. Unless she hits her head a few too many times on the way down, there is no way she'll believe any of that crud. My best hope is that she's so disoriented by the ride, I can overwhelm her with concern for her well-being. She might buy it.

Who am I trying to kid? My mom was broken in by Francis and perfected by Reese. She knows every excuse, reason, and rationalization that was ever whined by every kid who ever existed. There's no way to get past her.

Wait. I've got it. It's the perfect excuse that solves all my problems and makes everything right.

"<u>Reese</u> made me do it!"

CHAPTER TWELVE

On any other day, this would not look good. Flour on the floor, a broken egg in the sink, spilt milk on the counter. What would mean certain disaster for Dewey at any other time only meant fun today. After bonding over buttons, Dewey and his new best friend, Mrs. White, had baked cookies and the evidence remained scattered across the kitchen.

The two chocolate chip culprits sat together in Fort Dewey. So what if it was really a blue blanket stretched between a chair and the couch? To Dewey it was a fortress of chocolate solitude that he was sharing with Mrs. White.

"You're a lot more fun to play with than my brothers," Dewey said, nibbling on the edge of a cookie.

"Why's that?" Mrs. White asked and nibbled on her own Toll House.

"Because when I'm playing with my imaginary friend, Reese hits me and says I shouldn't talk to myself."

Mrs. White's eyes widened. "Reese sounds like a horrid little boy."

Dewey nodded eagerly. I have to agree with him on this one.

"You know," Mrs. White continued, "there's nothing wrong with having an imaginary friend. I talk to my Harold all the time."

"You do?" Dewey brightened.

"Of course. He's here right now."

"Would he like a cookie?" Dewey asked, reaching for a new treat.

"Sure," Mrs. White replied.

Dewey lifted the cookie and fed Harold for a moment, then Mrs. White tapped him on the shoulder.

"No. He's over there," she corrected and pointed to the other side of the fort.

Dewey fed Harold and Mrs. White wiped the crumbs from her lap. "Well, how would you like to liven things up a little?"

Dewey nodded enthusiastically. Maybe they were going to make brownies.

Mrs. White rose slowly. Her bones creaked like a rusty door. She strolled over to the stereo, turned it on, and cranked up the volume so loud, it's impossible to tell if she wanted to party or was half-deaf.

Mrs. White pulled a red rose from a vase and handed it to Dewey. Dewey placed it in his mouth and held it there as Mrs. White lifted him off the ground. Then my little brother and Mrs. White started to dance — the tango! Dewey's toes dangled two feet off the floor.

A song twenty years older than Dewey blasted through the house. Mrs. White and her young dance partner spun and twirled. Again. And again.

49

Faster and faster they spun. Mrs. White was cast back to long-lost memories when she had, like, a thousand less wrinkles.

The music pounded. The two dancers bounced. And then — well, let's just say it's a good thing Dewey was paying attention the day Mom taught him about 911.

Minutes later, Dewey watched sadly as the ambulance rushed Mrs. White to the hospital. He wondered if Harold had gone with her and hoped she could come back later to finish sorting the buttons and make more cookies.

As the screaming sirens faded in the distance, Dewey turned and saw a red balloon bounce down the street.

Now, I know that Dewey has seen hundreds of balloons in every color. In fact, if Dewey had stopped at that moment and done a little better job of deciding "Should I or shouldn't I?" he might have remembered that we still had a whole drawer of unused balloons from his last birthday party.

But Dewey's brain gave Dewey the wrong answer. He decided "I should" and chased the red balloon down the street.

Forty minutes later, Dewey finally looked up. He was in a strange neighborhood that might as well have been a different country. Our house, Mrs. White, and the red balloon were nowhere to be seen. If Harold was there, Dewey had no way of telling.

Given the overwhelming idea of being lost, Dewey pursued the only option his little mind could see.

He chased something else: a brown paper bag that was blowing down the street.

I'm a genius. At least that's what the test scores say. And I'm in the Krelboyne class at school with all the other little geniuses. And I have more homework than a doctor. How is it that being a genius doesn't automatically make you smart? You should totally be immune to stupidity and all things stupid.

That's my thinking, anyway.

Okay, so shoving my mom down a water slide at Wavetown USA may not have been the smartest thing to do. But what choice did I have? She had me and Reese dead on. And Reese had me in his sights, too. If she didn't get me, he was going to.

So what's a genius to do to get himself out of a jam? You got that right.

He's going to use his brain. And this time, my brain said, "Push."

Wait. "Push"? <u>That</u> was the sum total of my genius?

Maybe those test scores were wrong.

CHAPTER THIRTEEN

Dads are a tough bunch. They can drop things on their toes without cursing, watch an entire football game without a bathroom break, and eat anything in the fridge like a human garbage disposal.

And some dads are even tougher.

For them, it can take not one, not two, but three security guards to toss them out of a water park. That's *my* dad — he's a "three security guard" kind of guy.

"Wavetown USA doesn't need people like you," a burly guard screamed, his face as red as my dad's sunburned back.

"And *stay* out!" the burliest guard said.

"Now, when you say, 'Lifetime ban,' exactly whose lifetime are we talking about?" That's my dad. Always curious.

Mom dragged Reese and me by our shirt collars, just like a security guard would have if I'd pushed one down a water slide. "If it's one of these boys' lifetimes, then we'll see you tomorrow!"

These boys? This was better than I could have ever hoped. *I* pushed Mom down a water slide and Reese and I are splitting the punishment. Justice prevails!

"Ow! Mom! Please let my feet touch the ground!" Reese whined.

"I'll let your feet touch just as soon as you're old enough to send to prison."

"But —" was all that escaped Reese's mouth.

"Don't you ever ask me for anything. Ever." Mom was in the total Mom mode now. "I should have just given birth to chimps — at least then I could expect this kind of behavior." She yanked on my collar.

"Ow!" It was my turn to whine. My shirt rubbed against my sunburn. I thought about today and I thought about family outings and realized where I made my mistake.

I should have stayed home.

In a few short minutes, we were stuck inside my parents' van. And when I say stuck, I say it with a capital "uck." It was so hot the sweat glued my neck to the headrest, like gum to the floor of a movie theater.

"I'm hot," Reese moaned.

And you want to know the worst of it? It's hotter inside the van than it is outside. It's ninety-five degrees outside but it was like a million degrees in the van. Why? Because we have a crappy van, that's why. My dad has to run the heater so the car doesn't overheat.

Don't ask me. It makes sense to him.

"I think I'm getting heatstroke," Reese groaned louder this time. The temperature in the car was at least twice his IQ.

No, wait. That would only be seventy degrees, huh?

"Nonsense, you're still sweating," diagnosed Mom, the family doctor. "You've got at least another hour."

The car lurched sideways. I was too stuck to move, but I could feel my bare skin pull against the head-rest and stretch like taffy.

"Hal, stop swerving," Mom said. But Dad was too busy looking in the rearview mirror.

"This darn silver Toyota's been tailgating me for the last three miles," was Dad's only response.

"Then just pull over and let him pass," she instructed. "You're only going to make him mad."

"Oh-ho-ho! Flashing the brights!" Dad said to the mirror. "It's gonna be like that, is it?"

He stepped on the brake. Our van slowed and I heard the squeal of the tires from the silver Toyota. I braced for the crash.

"Hal!" Mom yelled. "Are you nuts? He could have a gun."

Dad finally turned to Mom. "Lois, I'm teaching the boys a lesson in manners. You won't get anywhere in life flashing brights at your problems."

But apparently you *will* get somewhere in life driving slow enough to make someone flash their brights at your problems.

"Just let him pass," she repeated.

Dad stared at Mom for a minute, then returned his gaze to the rearview mirror. "All right, silver Toyota," he sighed. "You win this round. But I'll be watching you, waiting for the next time."

Dad turned on the blinker and switched lanes. The little silver car gunned its engine and zoomed past like it was shot out of a cannon.

Dad leaned out the window yelling, "Go ahead! Get there two seconds sooner." He slumped down in the seat. "That guy is just an accident waiting to happen."

Before anyone in our van could agree or disagree, I heard the horn blast from one of those huge eighteen-wheel trucks ahead of us. Then tires screeched and there was that hideously cool sound of metal crunching against metal. Like, *gwaaanargghrrwaaaa!*

Dad stomped on the brakes and we skidded to a stop in front of the biggest and most awesome traffic wreck I'd ever seen — and that includes movies. And the best thing? I finally came unstuck from the seat.

Dad got out of the car and slammed the door. Mom did the same.

"Well, this is great. Just great," Dad said. "I'm going to miss the game."

"Is that all you can think about, Hal?" Mom asked. "You and your stupid sports?"

"Stupid? Why, I'll have you know that —" Dad stopped. He had seen it. Up ahead the silver Toyota was squished like a bug underneath a big eighteen-wheel truck. Although it was more like a thirteen-wheel truck now. And the car was more like a . . . well . . . did I already say squished bug?

The air soon filled with the sounds of police sirens and I saw a helicopter rise up over a nearby hill. Hey, this might not be such a bad day after all. Too bad Dewey had to miss this. He loves a nice car wreck.

CHAPTER FOURTEEN

Today, I actually envy Dewey. He's no genius, but at least he got to stay home and play with the baby-sitter. That means unlimited television, and you can eat whatever you can find in the refrigerator that's not rotted or tastes like vegetables.

But what I didn't know just then? Dewey's adventure was taking him well beyond "what's the green thing stuck to the bottom of the refrigerator?"

After Dewey got bored with the paper bag, and kicking the soda can, and chasing the afternoon breeze, he wandered off and found a friend to talk to, which, with my little brother, is usually exhausting to everyone but him.

"And then I was playing with the baby-sitter," Dewey said. "And we were singing and dancing and then she said, 'Where's my pills?' and then she fell over and the ambulance came, but there was this balloon and I was chasing it and then I didn't know where I was, and then I chased a paper bag, and then I *really* didn't know where I was, and then I saw you and I thought maybe you could help me."

The scarecrow in the middle of the cornfield said nothing. That didn't stop Dewey.

"Because you helped that little girl," he continued. "The one in the movie, you know. So, if you could just come to life and help me, I would really appreciate it."

The scarecrow still said nothing.

"You know, like in the movie."

Apparently, the scarecrow never saw the movie.

"Okay. Thanks anyway." Dewey shrugged and wandered deeper into the cornfield.

Minutes later, he found his way out of the cornfield and into the front seat of a lady farmer's beat-up old car.

Dewey sat in the passenger seat as it traveled down a dirt road next to the cornfield. Absent-mindedly, which for Dewey is pretty much 24/7, he sang. "A, b, c, d . . . a, b, c, d . . . a, b, c, d . . ."

Mrs. Elliott, the lady in the farmer overalls, was just as run-down as the car. She was taking my little brother . . . well, somewhere.

"You know," Mrs. Elliott started, "it's a good thing I found you. It's not very safe for a little boy like you to be all by himself."

"A, b, c, d . . . a, b, c, d . . ." Dewey sang.

"But don't worry," she continued. "I'll get you back home to your parents. They must be worried sick."

"A, b, c, d . . . a, b, c, d . . ." Dewey kept singing.

Mrs. Elliott had to be going crazy already. *A, b, c, d . . .* I wasn't even in the car and it's making *me* nuts! Dewey on his own is irritating enough. But man, you add some music and it's a quick step to "drive me crazy town."

"It's 'e,' dear. A, b, c, d, e."

"I know," Dewey replied, then continued singing, "A, b, c, d . . . a, b, c, d . . ."

Mrs. Elliott just smiled. Maybe she had kids of her own? If not, today would certainly change her mind.

CHAPTER FIFTEEN

While Dewey was driving strangers cuckoo, Francis sat around a table with Joe and Eric, other cadets at Marlin Academy. Following "The Great Billiard Shoot-out," the cadets were eager to find a new challenge. Or maybe they were bored. It's hard to tell sometimes.

Francis and his buddy Joe examined a box of tasty marshmallow "Quacks" while Eric quietly tried to read his newspaper.

Francis popped a Quack into his mouth. "Sugar, corn syrup, and gelatin. How can something so simple be so delicious?"

"That stuff's nasty, Francis," Joe said.

Francis held up another Quack and rolled it around on his fingertips like Shaq would a basketball. "To the unsophisticated palate, yes. But to me, a Quack is nature's perfect food. A duck-shaped, sugar-flavored nugget of powdery happiness." He popped the Quack into his mouth. "I bet I could eat a hundred of them."

"No way," Joe insisted. "All that marshmallow would expand in your stomach. You wouldn't get past fifty."

"That's where you're wrong, Joe," Francis calmly explained. "The marshmallow wouldn't expand. It would dissolve. I'd never get full. In fact, I don't think even a hundred Quacks are enough. I could probably —"

Eric was full of this Quack-enriched banter. He angrily crumpled his newspaper. "Will ... you ... just ... shut ... up!"

Francis popped another Quack in his mouth.

Eric added, "I have sat back and said nothing as you two have gone on and on about how you can eat a hundred of this and lift a hundred of that." He glared at Francis. "The Quacks would expand. You're an idiot if you think differently."

Uh-oh. I knew my brother. Francis wasn't going to let an insult like that fly by.

Francis calmly reached into the bag of Quacks and selected his next victim. "Let me explain something to you, Eric. If I say I can eat a hundred Quacks, you can take that as a bona fide guarantee. And there's no need to resort to personal attacks." He popped the Quack into his mouth. "Because I'd hate to raise the whole issue of you wearing boxer shorts in the shower."

"I don't care if I wear plate armor in the shower," Eric spat back. "You can't eat a hundred Quacks because the marshmallow would expand."

"Dissolve," Francis quipped.

Heck, I don't know if marshmallow would dissolve or expand, but in minutes, The Great Quack Attack expanded to include nearly a dozen cadets, split into two separate groups: The pro-Francis Dissolvers and the pro-Eric Expanders.

"Look," Francis explained, "my freshman year I ate seven pounds of grapes in one sitting. No bathroom break. I think I know what my body's capable of."

That's true. I once watched him eat an entire watermelon and then shoot out all the seeds with one mighty spit like a human machine gun. He's so cool.

"Francis, we're not talking grapes," Eric reasoned. "We're talking pure sucrose. The human body simply cannot absorb the sugar from a hundred Quacks."

The other Expanders nodded in agreement.

Cadet Finley didn't want to hear such negativity. He leaned around Francis to defend his champion. "Hey, in extreme cases, the human pancreas has been known to increase its insulin production by up to sixty percent."

The pro-Francis Dissolvers cheered the revelation.

"I'm premed," Finley announced to the group.

Eric wagged a finger in Finley's face. "Your pancreas can produce enough insulin to fill a swimming pool, but it won't mean squat if your adrenal gland can't distribute it into your bloodstream fast enough." Eric turned to the Expanders. "Prelaw."

Eric's Expanders cheered while the Dissolvers let out enough "boos" to fill a stadium. It was getting ugly. Either a fight or a hockey game was going to break out . . . and soon.

But Francis didn't want a fight. He wanted a victory.

And most of all, he wanted Quacks. He held out his arms like a Roman emperor. Both sides quieted down.

"Gentlemen, gentlemen," he said. "This argument is pointless. We could philosophize about this all night. But I'm not a philosopher. I'm a man of science."

Francis strolled over to a table piled high with enough Quacks to stop a diabetic train. He grabbed one off the top, tossed it casually into the air and caught it between his teeth, biting through the marshmallow. He gulped it down.

"One," he said.

I would have eaten a thousand <u>Quacks</u> if it would've gotten me out of this heat and far from this rotten traffic jam. The problem with a really cool traffic accident is that it has one stinky downside: It creates a very uncool traffic jam. And there's nothing like a traffic jam to totally ruin everyone's day.

Cars overheat, tempers flare, and there's a lot of yelling. Kind of like a Fourth of July cookout at our house.

So I'm stuck. I'm not at home and I'm not at the water park anymore. I'm in the one place that's not at all designed for kids — the middle of the freeway.

Parents are always saying, "Stay out of the street!" and "Don't play in traffic!" Now here I am in the street and in traffic and I can't wait to get out of here and get home. Or anywhere. To get out of this heat and out of this traffic jam, I'd even go to school and sit with my fellow Krelboynes.

How lame is that? Maybe this heat <u>has</u> gotten to my brain!

CHAPTER SIXTEEN

At least we got out of the van. Reese and I stood with our parents behind the yellow police tape and watched the emergency crews work. This was our own reality TV — like *Survivor* without the commercials.

"That was totally cool," Reese said. "Did you see the truck jackknife and flip over? And that giant tire fly through the air? An explosion would've been sweet, but you can't have everything."

"Yeah, Reese," I replied. "This is just great. Now we're stuck here for hours with no food, no air-conditioning." Of course, it could be worse. I could be the guy in what's left of the silver Toyota.

"Silver Toyota . . . silver Toyota," was all Dad could say. Mostly to himself, at least. Meanwhile, Mom decided to have a deep and meaningful discussion with one of the policemen.

"Why can't you just open one lane?" It was a question, but she phrased it like a demand.

"Lady, we have to wait for the crane to get here before we even think of opening the road to traffic," the policeman patiently explained.

But Mom had her own ideas. Did you guess that?

"All you have to do is move a couple of those police cars and there'd be enough room to pass on the shoulder," she insisted. "This is just plain stupid."

"Ma'am, don't call a police officer stupid."

"What, that's a law now?"

Mom should have known that. There seems to be a law for everything. Except for one against boredom. We'd been stuck in traffic for an hour already. I'd counted cars, put license plate numbers in numerical order, and identified several types of rash-inducing plants.

Yep. I'm bored.

My mom was totally happy, though. She'd found something to yell about and someone new to yell at about it. And for once, it wasn't me.

"Look, look right there," she said to Dad as she pointed to a road crew. "They're just standing around. Five hundred cars full of people who actually have places to go and they're just standing there talking? What is there to discuss?"

"Life. What does it all mean?" Dad shrugged.

Mom looked past the worker to the others and yelled, "Let me clear something up for you people. It's a car wreck. You're a road crew. Do your job!"

She turned her attention back to Dad. "You know, if they could handle a real job —" She paused and waved a hand in front of his eyes. "Are you even listening to me?"

"It could've been me," Dad said, referring to the accident.

"It could've been all of us, Hal," Mom said.

"Nope," Dad responded. "That silver Toyota got sliced right through the driver's seat. You and the boys would have walked away without a scratch. And that's the way I would've wanted it."

Is that gross or what? I hope I'm happier when I'm grown up. Heck, why wait until I'm grown up? I hope I'm happier tomorrow.

Reese tugged on my shirt and pointed down the line of idling cars. We left Angry Mom and Distressed Dad and walked through the traffic jam. "This totally reeks," I exclaimed. "It's like an oven out here. What's the point of walking aimlessly through traffic?"

"So we can find cool stuff like this," my brother responded as he picked up an old dirty sock from the road. He sniffed it. "Smells like gasoline."

That's my brother for you, overwhelmed by the ordinary. Fortunately, I need more than an old sock to keep me entertained.

Or maybe that's unfortunately?

"Can't we just go back to the van?" I whined. "My feet are kill —"

But Reese didn't hear me. He was already several feet ahead, running and pointing. There's only one thing that makes Reese behave like that, and it's not a lost Krelboyne.

"Ice cream man! Ice cream man!" he yelled.

I caught up with him at the ice cream truck. An ice cream man stood there, arms folded in front of some angry kids. Ice cream man? This guy looked more like the "I scream" man.

"Go away," the ice cream man said. "There is no ice cream in the truck."

One of the kids jumped up and peeked through the window. "He's lying. There's *tons* of ice cream in there!"

Mr. Ice Cream Man gritted his teeth. "The ice cream in the truck is not for sale. It is against the law for me to sell ice cream in the middle of traffic."

"But nothing's moving!" Reese explained. "Traffic moves. This is just a four-lane parking lot." Maybe he has a career in law ahead of him?

"What's your problem? Don't you like kids?" I followed up.

"Hey, I am an ice cream man, am I not?"

"You didn't answer the question. . . ." I insisted.

"This is just wrong," Reese offered. "You could make money and please children. This is a senseless act." He stuck his finger in the ice cream man's face. "You are evil. Pure evil."

"Wait right here," the ice cream man instructed. He turned around and walked into his truck. Slowly he rolled up the windows and then with a flick of the wrist locked all the doors.

"Son of a —!" Reese seethed.

"He's got us." I was hot, tired, and bored. And now I wasn't getting any ice cream. "There's nothing we can do."

"Oh yes there is."

I know what you're thinking. I was stunned, too. My brother actually sounded like he had a plan. Then I saw his plan in action. He dove headfirst into the truck's door and started banging on it with his forehead.

"And the Nobel Prize for science goes to . . ." a voice said from behind me. I turned and saw . . . her.

"That's my —" I started. Whoa! Was I defending Reese? Not today.

"Good one," I finished.

"I'm Jessica," she introduced herself and pointed across two lanes of traffic. "Gray Volvo."

"Malcolm," I offered. "Crappy minivan."

A girl? Talking to me? Maybe the heat had gotten to her? I had to figure out something to do next. Or say, even. While I wracked my brain for anything that sounded like conversation, she beat me to it.

"Do you want to go check out the crash site?"

"Sure," I responded. "You know, my dad practically caused it."

"Wow."

Cool. She's impressed. It's about time Dad did something useful.

CHAPTER SEVENTEEN

"Can you *believe* this mess?" I said to Jessica as we walked through the traffic jam. "We'll be stuck here all day!" We followed the skid marks on the freeway toward the flashing red lights up ahead. The cause of all of this, my dad, sat in our van listening to a medley of death songs on the radio as he stared straight ahead.

Whatever.

As we walked, we passed my mom, who was talking to a businessman in an Audi, which was pretty weird. Usually my mom just talks *at* people.

"Look, please," Mom begged. "Let me use your cell phone for just one minute."

"But I don't think —" Mr. Audi began.

"My six-year-old is home with a new baby-sitter and I have to call and let her know we'll be late."

"I'm sorry," he said. He held up the phone. "But the battery's dead. I wish I could help you."

Just then his dead cell phone rang. He looked at my mom and she looked at him. They both looked at the suddenly living cell phone. The man rolled up his car window in front of my fuming mother.

When Jessica and I got to the crash site, it was too late.

"Go on back to your cars." From behind the yellow police tape, a cop was doing his job: shooing away a bunch of kids from the crash site. "There's nothing to see here."

What's he talking about? This is the only thing to see for twenty miles. This stuff always happens to me. I'm stuck here, bored out of my mind, and when I find the one thing that's even a little bit interesting, they actually pay someone to keep me away from it.

"Well, that's that," I whined. "Let's go back." I started to turn and walk back to my parents' crappy mini-van, but Jessica grabbed my arm.

"Just follow me, Malcolm," she said.

A girl with a plan. I like that. A *lot*.

Jessica lifted the yellow tape. We both walked under it as the cop watched.

"And just where do you think you're going, young lady?" he demanded.

"It's okay," Jessica answered. "My dad's an investigator for the Department of Transportation. We're supposed to meet him here." She looked past the cop. "Oh, there he is! Hi, Daddy!" She waved.

A confused-looking man in a hard hat waved back tentatively.

"Okay," the cop said. We walked right past him.

"Wow," I said to Jessica. "Your dad's a crash investigator?"

"Here's a little secret, Malcolm," she whispered.

"When you want something, everybody's your dad."
She waved to another hard hat. "Hi, Daddy!"

He waved back, too. Okay, she's cute, she's smart, she fibs to cops . . . I just may be in over my head here.

CHAPTER EIGHTEEN

My mom had found a call box by the side of the freeway and had dragged Dad over to create some shade.

"Okay, I'll hold," she said into the phone, and positioned Dad to block out the sun.

"Think about it, Lois. I stopped to tie my shoe in the parking lot at Wavetown. If I hadn't done that, we would have gotten on the road twenty seconds sooner. I would have been two hundred yards ahead of where I was. And then I would have been the silver Toyota."

"Yeah," Mom responded. "And if Malcolm and Reese hadn't pushed me down the water slide, and if the three of us hadn't landed on the mayor and hadn't gotten ejected from the park, we'd still be there. It's all an intricate tapestry, Hal." Then she turned her attention to the phone. "Yes, hello? Did you ask your supervisor?"

"Yes, ma'am," the operator replied. "And this phone is for emergency roadside assistance only. I can't connect you to a private line."

"Look, I have to get through to my baby-sitter. Just

let me talk to your supervisor." Like all moms, my mom never took no for an answer when she wanted yes. Which was, like, all the time.

"One moment, ma'am," the operator said. "I'll put you through." After a pause, a mysterious, deeper voice came over the phone. "Hello, this is the supervisor."

"No, it isn't," Mom said. "You're just disguising your voice." I could have told him that trick wouldn't work. Reese and I quit trying that one last summer.

"No. I really am the supervisor."

"You can't do this!" my mom yelled.

"Ma'am, I'm about to be replaced by a machine that costs $3.29 and is made in Taiwan. I can do whatever I want. What are you going to do about it?"

I'll tell you what my mom did about it. She pounded the phone against the side of the call box. The sunlight broke on her face. "Hal!" Dad moved slightly to block out the sun.

Reese and the other ice-cream-demanding kids stood in front of the ice cream truck and glared through the windshield at the ice cream man inside.

The ice cream man grinned evilly as he held up an ice cream cone and wrapped his tongue around it like a dog with a Milk-Bone. He continued smiling as he flipped a switch on the dashboard. A second later, the familiar ice cream song, the siren call for ice cream lovers worldwide, started playing at full volume.

Man, that guy is cruel!

The kids seethed. Reese charged the ice cream truck and bashed it with his head, again. If there had been a brain in there, I'm sure it would have hurt.

CHAPTER NINETEEN

The exasperated Mrs. Elliott and Dewey drove down a country road and turned onto the freeway — in this case the "freeway" meant the only two-lane paved road for miles around.

"What time is it?" Dewey asked.

"It's still four o'clock," she struggled to say sweetly. "You have to wait at least a minute before the time changes, dear."

That's Dewey all right. He's got a million questions and half a million are the same one. The other half million are just annoying.

"What time is it in China?"

See what I mean?

"Well, sweetie," Mrs. Elliott replied, "I think they're a good twenty hours or more —"

"Do you speak Chinese?" Dewey interrupted.

"No I don't, but —"

"Why not?"

"Well, I didn't —"

"Is Chinatown in China?"

"Honey, if you want the answer to a question, you have to first wait for —"

"Do they eat beets in China?"

"I think —"

"What does this toe do?" Dewey asked, pointing to his shoe. I don't think Dewey really needs to breathe, so waiting for the answers was just wasting time.

"You know what?" Mrs. Elliott finally said. "I need to buy some cigarettes. . . ." She turned the wheel of her car and swung a speedy U-turn into the nearest 7-Eleven. ". . . for the first time in twenty years."

The car screeched into the parking lot and took up three spaces and a piece of the sidewalk. Mrs. Elliott leaped from the car, leaving Dewey behind. For an old lady, she still had some bounce in her bunioned feet.

"Grape juice, please," Dewey called after her, adding, "How many grapes in grape juice?"

Okay — this is when things got a little crazy.

She ran into the store at the same exact moment that Chuck Johannson ran *out*, carrying a rack filled with bags of potato chips. There was something about him that screamed "thief." It could have been the ski mask. Or the owner of the store chasing after him, yelling, "Stop, thief!"

Chuck opened Mrs. Elliott's car door, threw the rack of potato chips into the backseat, and plopped in the driver's seat. He revved the engine and squealed the tires out of the parking lot.

Chuck pulled off the mask, laughing as he looked in the rearview mirror. Then he heard the sound. The unmistakable crunch of Mesquite Barbecue

Potato Chips. He looked over the backseat and saw Dewey with a large open bag.

"Hello," Dewey said. "Did you get my grape juice?"

A startled Chuck lurched in the seat and smacked his head on the roof. He hit the brakes and the car skidded over to the side of the road. Dewey can do that to you.

"How much do ants weigh?" Dewey asked, his tiny brain still full of unanswered questions. "Are we going to China?"

Chuck took one look at Dewey's innocent face and sighed. Dewey held out a bag of sea-salt-and-vinegar chips.

"Do you like chips?"

"Kid," Chuck said, "I can't get enough of 'em!" Chuck took a chip and stomped on the accelerator, easing the car back onto the freeway.

Ten minutes later, Chuck and Dewey were like best friends. That's what happens with Dewey — you either share his world or it drives you crazy.

Chuck turned Mrs. Elliott's car off the freeway and into a residential neighborhood. Inside, he poured out his criminal heart to Dewey.

"And when you're constantly moving from town to town, it's really hard to make friends," he said. "So, yeah, I acted out my feelings, I guess, but who wouldn't in my situation?"

The only sound from Dewey was the crunch of potato chips. Nacho-cheese-flavored, this time.

"The first thing I ever stole was a 'World's Greatest

Dad' mug," Chuck added. "I never once saw him drink his coffee out of it."

Dewey continued chewing as the sounds of police sirens came from behind them. Chuck looked in the rearview, then quickly pulled the car over to the side of the road.

"All right, little buddy, I'm going to have to let you off here."

"Okay," Dewey replied.

The car came to a stop and Dewey got out carrying a big bag of sour-cream-and-onion.

"*Vaya con Dios*, Dewey," Chuck said. "Now, don't you worry. I'm not going to let them take me alive. *That'll* get my dad's attention!"

Chuck stomped on the gas and the car sped off. Two police cars whizzed after him. Dewey crunched another chip.

Crunch completed, Dewey looked around and saw a group of migrant workers standing on the sidewalk. He walked over and offered them some chips. A pickup truck pulled up and the driver held out four fingers. Three workers and Dewey climbed into the back of the truck and the truck drove off down the street, Dewey, potato chips, and all.

CHAPTER TWENTY

By the time Jessica and I got to the actual crash, there was nothing cool to see. A crushed truck, a crumpled car, a street littered with broken glass. None of the really good stuff.

Isn't that the way it always is? I could probably see more on the news and see it over and over again in slow motion.

"The cop was right," I complained. "There really is nothing to see here."

That didn't stop Jessica. She grabbed my hand and started climbing a nearby hill.

"You have to check out this view, Malcolm. It's great!"

Oh great. That's what I need. Scenery. Right now, I was busy battling a pricker bush that was stabbing my arms and catching my pants.

"Could someone please tell me what Mother Nature was thinking of when She created the pricker bush?"

"Maybe She wanted to slow us down to enjoy the great outdoors, Malcolm," Jessica offered.

This is what's wrong with the great outdoors. There are too many things that can hurt you.

"Ouch!" I yelped as a pricker snuck its way through my sock. This whole being-outside thing was too much for me. I needed a candy bar, a comfortable place on the sofa, and a few mindless hours in front of the television.

"I hate pricker bushes. What fruit are they trying to protect anyway? Do you see *anything* on this shrub worth protecting?" I had almost as many questions as Dewey. It had to be the heat. "What are we doing up here?"

"Just enjoying the sights," she said as she reached the top. She gestured across the bottom of the hill.

What I saw was a total Kodak moment. A Kodak moment that almost brought tears to my eyes. I saw Reese jumping up and down on the roof of the ice cream truck, screaming and yelling at the ice cream man inside.

"And check out that crazy lady over there," Jessica giggled.

She was pointing at . . . my mom! She'd totally blown her cool, too, and was "Reesing" the emergency call box, ripping off the receiver and hurling it over the guardrail. I needed a quick diversion before my family lineage was discovered.

"Let's look at something else," I cleverly said. "Hey, wow, a pricker bush. Why, just look at that!"

Thank you, Mother Nature!

"So tell me about this gifted class you're in," she requested, ignoring the prickers. Jessica was not easily distracted.

84

"It's horrible," I whined. "Every day I'm surrounded by Krelboynes who are not at all normal. I have twice as much homework as anyone in my grade and I have to take all these college prep classes —"

"Oh, what a total nightmare for you. If you're not careful, you might get a full scholarship to Harvard."

She was mocking me! "You don't understand."

"I certainly do," she said. "Malcolm, you've done nothing but bellyache nonstop for the last hour and a half. Why don't you try to be happy for, like, thirty seconds?"

I was shocked. "We've been stuck here for an hour and a half?"

"Okay. Starting now," she said. "I'm serious. All you do is complain."

"I happen to complain the perfect amount for someone in my situation." And that's true. I did the research. "Today is a perfect example. I mean, look at this mess. What's good about this? The traffic jam, the heat?"

I had her. No one could find *anything* good in this. She was giving it serious thought. "Well," she finally said. "If it weren't for this . . . we never would have met."

Okay! Could someone please turn off the "loser" sign flashing on my forehead? I couldn't do anything but look at her. And then I noticed she was looking at me.

Her.

Me.

She moved closer.

I moved closer.

Closer.

Closer still.

Jessica smiled. Was she going to ...? Yes ... I think she is ... I closed my eyes and ... Yow!

She shoved me down the hill!

Is this girl incredible or what?

I rolled down the hill like a soda can thrown from a moving car. I had to stop myself before I hit some rocks below. I reached out and grabbed a tree root. Well, I thought it was a tree root.

"Yeow!" I screamed. "Prickers!"

The thing about Jessica is that she's just as smart as a Krelboyne, but she's normal. She can talk. She can laugh. We have similar interests. And I like spending time with her.

I can't say that about any of the girl Krelboynes in my class.

Maybe this wasn't so bad. Mom had found someone to yell at. Dad got some time to himself. Reese found something to assault. And I found Jessica.

Maybe traffic accidents aren't so bad after all.

CHAPTER TWENTY-ONE

"**Y**ou guys have purpose," Dad said. He stood next to a motorcycle cop, talking out loud like somebody cared. I couldn't believe the cop was still awake. I wouldn't be.

". . . and I keep rolling it around in my head," Dad said. "How much time do I have left, and what have I done with my life?" He pointed to the cop. "You go home at night knowing you've made the world a better place, forging that thin blue line . . . and that's real, man. If I could just once feel that sense of accomplishment . . . Do you know how special you are? Do you?"

The cop took one long look at my dad. Within seconds, dad was standing on one foot with his arms outstretched.

"Z . . . y . . . x . . . w . . . v . . . Officer, I have *not* been drinking."

"Let's just stick to the alphabet, sir," the officer responded. "Then we'll see if you can touch your nose with your index finger."

Mom had not given up on her plan to end the traffic jam and get the cars moving again. She was nagging — make that screaming at — several workers as they stood in front of a crane.

"Let me get this straight," she said. Of course, I knew that even once she got it straight, there would still be no peace and then she'd have to get it straighter. "We had to wait all afternoon for the crane, and now the crane is here."

"That's right, ma'am," the worker agreed.

"And the guy who works the crane, he's here, too."

"That's right."

"Then why is nothing happening?!"

"Look, lady, we can't touch anything until the investigators sign off on the crash report."

"Well, they must have been done hours ago," Mom reasoned. "Where are they?"

"That's a whole different department. It's really not my job to know."

So, *that* was supposed to make my mom happy? This guy had *no* idea who he was dealing with. I could have saved everybody a lot of time and trouble, but does anyone ever ask me? Nooooo.

"Start . . . the . . . crane," she demanded. If she'd had horns, now would be the time when they'd grow out of her head.

"You can't tell me what to do, ma'am. You're not my supervisor and you're not my mother or my wife."

What a lucky man.

*　　*　　*

Inside his truck, the ice cream man polished off another Dreamsicle and read about the "Scoop of the Month" in his copy of *Ice Cream Weekly*, the official publication of the National Ice Cream Federation. He looked up when he heard the scratching.

At the back of the truck, Reese had put a new plan into action. And this one actually made some sense. He had a crowbar wedged into the padlock and was about to give it a final twist. But Reese was stopped in mid-yank and the crowbar was pulled from him by a chubby hand.

"Not so fast, kiddo," the fat man said to Reese. With his other chubby hand, he grabbed my brother by the shirt collar.

"Let go of me," Reese demanded as only a whiny kid can.

Reese was still squirming as the ice cream man exited the truck and ran around to the back. "What is going on here?" he demanded.

"I'm Claude Wells," the fat man said. "This unruly child was trying to break into your truck."

"Let me go," Reese yelped. "I just want some of that ice cream. He's keeping it all to himself!"

"It's his ice cream," the fat man pointed out. "If he doesn't want to sell it, you can't make him."

"That is correct," the ice cream man agreed. He pointed to Reese. "You do not deserve ice cream," he lectured my brother, as sternly as anyone's mother.

"Yeah?" Reese replied. "Well, you don't deserve to be an ice cream man!"

"You take that back!" The ice cream man was hurt. "Or I am calling the cops!"

Reese stomped on Mr. Wells's foot. The fat man dropped to the ground and Reese ran off.

"Ow! Come back here, you little punk!" Mr. Wells screamed. He ran after Reese.

"Ha! That will teach you to mess with me!" the ice cream man yelled at Reese. "I was a surgeon in my country!"

The former surgeon and now ice cream man happily strolled back to the front of his truck. He stepped in and saw nothing. Nothing inside the truck, I mean. It was empty. The treasure of frozen delights was gone.

"No! I have been robbed!"

CHAPTER TWENTY-TWO

Francis sat at a table surrounded by both the Expanders and the Dissolvers. The pile of Quacks was noticeably smaller. Francis paused to lick Quack remains from his lips. He took a deep breath and sucked down yet another duck-shaped treat.

"Told you I could do this," he bragged.

"You haven't done it yet," Eric chastised. Man, that guy is tough!

But Francis just smiled and scooped up a handful of Quacks and shoved them into his mouth.

"Forty-six . . . forty-seven . . . forty-eight . . ." the cadets started counting again.

Francis was still smiling at fifty. He was pretending to smile at seventy-five. Finally, at one hundred Quacks, he couldn't smile if a crane lifted the sides of his mouth. But he did manage to push the final Quack between his lips.

"He did it! One hundred Quacks!" one of the Dissolvers yelled.

"A new record!" cried another one.

A Polaroid flash went off in front of Francis's face. This was a moment to preserve for the Academy's history books. Eric approached Francis and shook his hand.

"You've got heart," Eric said. "I would've given out around eighty-two."

"Way to go, Francis," Joe cheered. "That was way cooler than the time Davis did a thousand sit-ups."

Eric turned to Joe. "Impossible," Eric disagreed. "I mean Davis is in good shape, but a thousand sit-ups? You're begging for a double hernia."

"It's that kind of small-minded thinking that keeps you from recognizing true greatness."

Suddenly, the cadets had a new cause. Sides were chosen, insults and dares were shouted at increased volumes. Francis and the 100-Quack chow-fest were forgotten quicker than my mom's birthday.

"Not only that, but I could do a thousand sit-ups in less than thirty minutes," Joe bragged.

"No way."

"Way!"

"Prove it!"

"I will! Follow me!"

They continued arguing as they stepped over Francis and headed toward the gym.

Francis lay on the ground. His stomach looked like he'd eaten a basketball and his face was smeared with Quack residue.

"Oooohhhh," he moaned, just before letting out a sad, gurgling belch.

He won't be doing any sit-ups for a while, I'm guessing.

CHAPTER TWENTY-THREE

Reese squatted behind a FedEx truck, surrounded by his horde, his stolen treasure of ice cream. His newfound friends gathered around as he handed out boxes of frozen treats.

"Pleasure working with you, Kyle," he said. "Nice moves out there, Carlton."

A large shadow loomed over him and around the corner came . . . Mr. Wells. He cleared his throat and Reese turned to him.

"And here's your share, Mr. Wells," my brother said. "You were awesome."

Mr. Wells ripped open the top of his box, unwrapped an ice cream sandwich, and shoved it in his mouth with the grace of a fat dolphin. "That horrible man left us no choice."

Far away from Reese and his ice cream treasure, the crane sat in the center of the accident. Its hook jerked down, stopped, then jerked up again. If it was going nowhere, it was sure going there fast. Mom sat behind the controls of the giant construction crane, pressing buttons like a crazy monkey in a banana factory.

Outside the crane, the workers enjoyed the show. Some were even making bets.

"Try the green one!"

"Push the lever forward!"

"Hit any two buttons at the same time!"

Mom hit every button, some two or three times. Then she pounded the buttons just to make sure. And if she'd had a hammer . . . I think you get the picture. Nothing worked.

Occasionally, the crane lurched forward, then lurched right back where it started. If it was a lock on my door, Mom could've cracked its secret code within seconds. But the mysteries of the construction crane remained hidden inside its yellow-and-green metal body. Finally, a cop opened the crane door.

"Okay, ma'am," he said. "You've had your fun. Come on out of there."

"You order them to move this thing!" she demanded.

"Let's just get you out of the nice crane and then we'll have a little talk about what I should and shouldn't do." He talked to my mom like my dad talks to Grandma when it's time for her green pill.

"Don't you dare patronize me," she responded.

"Okay. You don't want to be patronized. I'll be blunt." The cop put his hands on his hips. That's never a good sign. "You're a control freak, lady. I see people like you all the time. But guess what? This is a traffic jam. It's out of your control."

"Yes but —"

"You can't boss it around. You can't yell at it and expect it to listen."

"I don't —"

"It will end when it ends and you're just going to have to live with it. There's absolutely nothing — let me repeat that — *nothing* you can do about it."

Check and mate! No one's *ever* talked to my mom like that — and lived to tell about it. Mom looked at the cop and then stomped away. As she stomped she passed a blue station wagon. Inside the locked car was a panting dog.

"And whose dog is this?" Mom yelled.

Everybody looked at the crazy, yelling lady and shrugged.

"I said whose dog is this?!" she repeated. "He's trapped in here with the windows rolled up and it's ninety degrees out!"

She waited. Well, she waited for as long as an angry mom will wait. Which is really not waiting at all.

"Fine," she said. "If this is nobody's dog, I guess nobody will care when I do this."

She leaned down and picked up a rock. Then she hauled back and let it fly. It smashed the car window. She held out her arms to the dog inside.

"Come on, sweetie," she said to the dog. "Don't be scared. Everything's all —"

The dog growled at her and leaped out of the car,

knocking Mom back. She screamed as the dog ran off.

Dad sat by the side of the road. I haven't seen him this upset since Reese tried to flush Dewey. Except for that time *I* tried to flush Dewey.

"Cooo," came the pathetic cry from his right side. He turned and saw a little pigeon wrapped up in one of those plastic six-pack holders. It was struggling to break free.

"Poor thing," Dad said. He thought for a moment, then looked to the sky. "I get it! I was hoping I could deliver a baby in a taxicab or something, but a life is a life!"

Dad untangled the pigeon and held it in his hands. He kissed it on the forehead. Like, gross!

"There you go, little guy," he said as he released the pigeon to the air. "Fly away! Be free! Live!"

At that exact moment, the newly freed dog raced past Dad and jumped into the air, growling. Man! I never saw so many feathers fly! It was like bird confetti.

Dad brushed some feathers off his shirt, shrugged, sighed, and walked away. I hope he's looking for another bird!

CHAPTER TWENTY-FOUR

I've got the whole first-aid thing down. With three brothers, two of them older, I've learned a lot about it over the years. And the one thing I know you need is a Band-Aid. Jessica and I stood next to her gray Volvo. She put one of the expensive nonstick name-brand ones on my prickered arm.

"I'm impressed. You actually have a working first-aid kit," I said. "We had one of those once, but my brother ate all the Band-Aids and used all the gauze for a game of Mummy's Curse."

She finished sticking it to my arm. "There you go, Malcolm. Good as new." She closed the kit and tossed it in the Volvo's trunk. It was now or never.

"You know, Jessica, I was thinking. All things considered, this was a pretty cool afternoon. Maybe sometime we could do something else. Maybe when we get back we —"

But I didn't have a chance to finish. Jessica slammed down the trunk and I saw it. Big as life. It took the wind right out of me just like that time Reese punched me. Okay, just like *all* those times Reese punched me. I couldn't believe it. There, right under the trunk, was her license plate: "Nova Scotia: Canada's Ocean Playground."

"You're from Canada?"

"We're here on vacation," she said.

Canada? Well, it could be worse. She could be French.

I was stunned. "Why didn't you tell me?"

"Because you would have spent the whole day grousing about it."

"No, I wouldn't have." Of course I would. "I knew this was too good to be true. I mean, why should I get to meet someone who's smart, funny, definitely not a Krelboyne, and not a member of my family?"

"But we *did* meet, Malcolm," she answered. "It was awesome. You know, it's okay to enjoy something even if it's just for a little while. Come on, admit it, we had fun today."

"No we didn't."

"You just said we did."

"Yeah, but that was before I knew it was all a big waste of time." It was like eating a whole box of Cracker Jack and there's no toy surprise. I mean, I know the toy surprises are lame and totally stupid, but I guess my point is . . . I don't know what my point is anymore.

Before I could say anything else, parents' voices filled the air.

"Suzie! Come back to the car, honey."

"Bobby! Let's get a move on, sport."

And then there was my mom's ear-piercing scream. "Malcolm! Reese! Moooove it!"

I looked at Jessica. "I gotta go."

"See ya, Malcolm."

This stinks. The worst. I slowly walked back to the van and all I could think about was how much I hated Cracker Jack. Reese ran by, chased by the dog. He dropped the boxes of melting ice cream and jumped into the van. The dog stopped chasing him and ate the ice cream instead.

Everybody loves ice cream.

Dad started the van and we moved slowly past the accident and down the freeway. I didn't even mind that the heater was on or that I was stuck to the headrest again. I had more important things on my mind. Then I heard a voice. Her voice.

"Malcolm!"

Jessica! I looked up and saw her gray Volvo. It had pulled alongside our van. Jessica leaned out the window, holding a piece of paper.

"Call me!" she yelled. Her phone number was on that paper. How cool is that!

I peeled myself away from the headrest. I shoved my arm out the window but I couldn't reach. Why do kids have such short arms? How fair is that?

"Malcolm! Get back inside the car this instant!" Mom yelled, like she knew what was good for me. I knew what was good for me — Jessica's phone number.

I stretched more, hoping my arm would grow.

Jessica stretched.

Finally! Our hands met over the dotted white line of the freeway. Pretty cool, huh? We clutched the paper between us. I was just about to be totally happy. Can you believe that?

That's when my world fell apart. Remember that stupid dog Mom let out of that car? The one that knocked her over, devoured Dad's bird, and ate Reese's ice cream? Well, that same stupid dog jumped between Jessica and me and snagged her phone number. He gulped it down like it was Puppy Chow and leaped over a guardrail, never looking back.

What happened to kennels? What about leash laws? Wild dogs running loose on freeways? Has the world gone insane? I hate dogs!

Within seconds, the gray Volvo had pulled ahead of us and I could see Jessica through the back window. She shrugged and waved good-bye.

Inside the van, Mom was miserable. She doesn't do well in traffic jams. Dad was still bummed out. He doesn't like traffic accidents. And Reese was totally mad. He really wanted that ice cream. Despite losing Jessica's phone number, I was surprisingly happy.

"That was great, wasn't it?" They all looked at me like I had three eyes. "Who would have thought a traffic jam would be so cool? We should totally do this again. When are we taking another road trip?"

Everybody in the car started laughing. I didn't think it was *that* funny.

CHAPTER TWENTY-FIVE

Dewey stood in the strawberry patch with the other migrant workers. He picked berries and put them in a giant basket, which he carried over to a flatbed truck. When someone blew a whistle, Dewey lined up with the other men single file. When he got to the front of the line, he was handed an envelope full of cash for the afternoon's work.

As Dewey walked back to the pickup truck for the return trip to the freeway, he passed the parked tour bus for the heavy metal band The Piltdowns. The band members all got out to stretch their legs. Dewey liked big shiny metal buses and this one was pretty big and awfully shiny. He got on board.

Hours later a motorcycle gang roared down our street. The Harleys were revving enough to make even our nicest neighbors complain — and we didn't *have* any nice neighbors. The Harleys stopped in front of our house and Dewey hopped off the cycle of a large gray-bearded biker.

"Good-bye, Santa," Dewey said as the gang roared off.

"Later, Dewey," the bearded one said. "You be good."

The bikers turned the corner just as our van passed them. We pulled into our driveway. Dewey was waiting for us.

"Dewey!" Mom called out as she jumped from the van.

"Hi, Mom."

Mom looked around. "Dewey, where's the baby-sitter?"

"She went away, then I drove off with a nice lady, and then a potato chip man, then —"

Mom started walking toward the house. "You got rid of another baby-sitter? Honestly, what's wrong with you kids?"

Reese smacked Dewey's shoulder and I mussed up his hair, both of us congratulating him on a job well done. Usually it takes all three of us to get rid of a sitter.

"And then I picked apples, then I played the drums in a band, and then we all went to jail, and —"

Banned for life from a water park. Witness to an awesome accident. Stuck for hours in a traffic jam on the hottest day of the year.

So when do I get a vacation to recover from my vacation?

At least I finally went down the Liquidator. Even if it was because Mom pulled me. And I met a pretty cool girl.

All the way home I kept thinking about the day and all the stuff Jessica said. Suddenly I was staring out the window totally zoned. Oh man! I've been spending too much time with my dad.

But like I said, what's the point? I've got this total nagging feeling that I'm missing something here. Maybe everything doesn't stink as much as I think. But Jessica lives on the moon, the dog ate her phone number, and all I have is this annoying pain in my butt.

A pain in my butt? Great. I probably hurt something. Can you break your butt?

I couldn't figure out what the heck it was. Then I get home and find a final pricker thorn stuck into my butt from when Jessica pushed me down the hill.

I pulled it out and dropped it into the top drawer of my desk. It fell into a scattered pile of Cracker Jack toy surprises and slid into the corner as I pushed the drawer shut.

I'm sure one day Dewey will stick it in his ear.

INTRODUCING THE NEW
Malcolm in the Middle
BOOK SERIES, BASED ON THE HIT TV SHOW!

MALCOLM IN THE MIDDLE #1: LIFE IS UNFAIR

MALCOLM IN THE MIDDLE #2: WATER PARK

MALCOLM IN THE MIDDLE: MY CLASS PROJECT

AVAILABLE NOW AT A BOOKSTORE NEAR YOU!
www.scholastic.com

◢ SCHOLASTIC

MAL1000